C000109011

"You have to go to sleep, my little ones. Or Santa won't be able to come and give you presents. You want your presents, don't you?"

"We want presents!" Dustin called from his bed, bouncing under the heavy blankets.

"Presents are nice, I guess. But Mama, we wanna meet Santa!" Lucy was the oldest. And she was also the most curious. Always asking her Mama questions, like a smart girl.

"We all wanna meet Santa, sweetie. But maybe, if you're good, Santa will visit you in your dreams."

"Mama, did you ever meet Santa?" Dustin calls, bouncing all over the bed in his Christmas Elf pajamas.

"Well, climb under those blankets kiddo, and I'll tell ya."

"You met Santa, Mama?" Lucy asks, tugging on her mother's sleeve with a big smile. The little girl was hopeful.

"I sure did, Lucille. Lemme tell you all about it. When I was a little girl, no older than Dustin is now-"

"I'm six and a half!" Dustin yelled, waving his favorite stuffed tiger through the air.

"You sure are bud!" Mama says. She sits down in a big red rocking chair and begins to tell a story.

"When I was six and a half, I took a trip to see Grandpa Woodsy, that's your Great Grandpa. He lived far away back then, on a super tall mountain. Sooooo tall that you couldn't see the top. And the mountain had lots of little fluffy clouds. It was so beautiful. So high up that only big birds lived up there. Birds the size of cars! And during the winter, the whole mountain was covered in bright green trees. I took a trip to the mountain to see Great-Grandpa just before Christmas. I didn't like the mountain when I was little. It was always so quiet."

"How'd you get to the top of the mountain, Mama?" Dustin asked.

"I had to climb. I'd jump on top of the big rocks. Like a billy goat! Baaa!" Their Mama told them.

"All by yourself?" Lucy asked.

"No way, Jose! I'd climb with the goats. And Great-Grandpa Woodsy! Nana and Pop would drop me off at the bottom of the big stone giant. That's what Grandpa Woodsy called the mountain!"

"Was it really a giant, Mama?"

"Well, that depends. What's the gift?"

"Come on, and I'll show you."

I climbed down into the hole that led beneath the house. That is where we house-elves live, you see. Under the floorboards, in the walls. Odd places, but we find them cozy and warm. And in my little cubby under the floor, I had a bunch of things I wanted to give my family.

"You see, it's against the House Elf Rules for stuff to just appear the way I want it to. But that's only on most days."

"And today is Christmas." Maple said, knowing where I was heading. "It's magical. So, things can appear, and it wouldn't break your rules, right?"

"That's right! You're one sharp Christmas cookie. Over the years, I've collected a lot of things for my family. I didn't know if I'd ever get the chance to give it to them, but I kept them. Just in case!"

"And now you want me to help you? But what can I do?"

"Well, I have to do a lot. I got all these candles you see. I want to get them lit and put them around the house. And I carved all these little nutcracker soldiers. I know they aren't as good as the ones you'd make, but-"

"No! Sniff, these are beautiful." Maple took one of my nutcrackers in her tiny hands, turning him over.

"Oh, you really think so? I painted them with wild berries. That's why their coats are all different colors. Some of them are red, and some of them are blue. Some are even purple!"

"They're very pretty." The Christmas elf said, smiling at me. She had bright rosy cheeks and short blond hair that touched her shoulders. I thought she was very pretty too. Even though she was a bit bigger than I was.

"Golly, Maple. Thanks so much. I've also got gifts that I found outside."

"You went outside of your house?"

"Yeah! I know it is against the House Elf Rules, but it was for my family. They work so hard; I think they deserve this."

"You really love your family, don't you?"

"Yeah! They're the nicest family I've ever had. I've been to other houses, but this one is the best. They're so sweet to each other. They hardly ever make a mess, and they always laugh or sing together. I want them to know I love them. And since I can't tell them, I figured I'd show them."

"But what if they don't know these are from you?"

"Well, that's okay! They'll know someone loves them very much. And that's all that matters."

"Alright, I've decided. I'll help you." Maple said, nodding her head, making the bells on her hat jingle. "Let's get to business! We don't have much time."

And so, on that Christmas Eve, Maple the Christmas Elf and I worked hard together. House elf and Christmas elf, side by side. We placed the candles on platters around the house and lit them. Now it wasn't just the fire that filled the house with light. The whole house was glowing a soft orange! We took my nutcracker soldiers and put them all over. Some on the fireplace and some under the Christmas tree. We set up a little display of them in rows on the dining table and surrounded them with more candles. We took the glass orbs that I had collected and put them on the Christmas tree. They looked so pretty, sparkling in the candlelight. We strung old garland across the ceiling. When it was done, we started to swing from strand to strand, like they were sparkly vines in a Christmas jungle.

"Alright, it's time to put the gifts beneath the tree. So, what did you get them, Sniff?"

"Well, Papa has always wanted to play music. So, I found him this old horn. I've polished it up with oil, so it should play really nice. And even though the Mama makes pretty clothes for everyone else, I know she's always wanted a long gown of her own. So, I got this out of the attic for her. It's old and has a few holes from moths, but I think she can fix them."

"Oh, it's so beautiful, Sniff! So elegant and such a pretty silver color. And the horn! It must have taken you a long time to polish off all the rust and make it shine. What did you get the children?"

"Well, George wants to build things when he becomes a full-sized Big Folk. So, I found him this hammer and screwdriver, and a wood chisel! And Molly wants to explore the world on a boat. So, I found her this fancy hat and old telescope. The hat has some holes, and the telescope needs a new lens. But she's a smart girl. I bet she'll fix it!"

"Oh Sniff. You know what? Maybe you're half Christmas elf. You've got a real gift for giving gifts." She smiled at me, and I almost started crying happy tears. That was the nicest thing anyone had ever said to me.

"Ah, Maple! Thank you. I couldn't have done this without you. Do you really think that they will like the gifts?"

"I think they will LOVE them."

We smiled at each other, and then we wrapped the gifts up real nice. I was worried I wouldn't be able to wrap them since I didn't have any wrapping paper. But Maple said a good Christmas elf always carries some. And she was the best Christmas elf. And then, once the gifts were all nice and dressed, we put them under the tree together.

"Well, that's the last of it. I better get back up to the roof and let Santa know he's good to come on down. It was really nice meeting you, Sniff!"

I couldn't think of anything to say. So, I hugged Maple and squeezed her tight. She was bigger than me, so I could only hug her waist, but she hugged me back.

"Will you come back next Christmas, Maple the Christmas Elf? We can do this again."

"Maybe I will, Sniff the House Elf. Maybe I will. Until then, Merry Christmas!"

And then she vanished in a cloud of silver dust. When the next morning came around, the tree had so many presents under it, my family didn't know what to do. George laughed and Molly screamed. The Mama and the Papa started to cry happy tears when they saw how beautiful the house looked. George really liked seeing all the nutcrackers lined up on the table. Molly started singing a sweet song about decked halls when she saw the garland hanging from the ceiling. I watched through the walls, doing a little dance of my own. I was so happy to be a part of their Christmas!

"Look, Mama! Papa! These presents are different from the rest."

"You're right, Molly. Good eyes." The Papa said, patting his daughter on the head and pulling out the gifts.

"Look, darling. The wrapping is different." The Mama said to him, touching his shoulder gently.

"Yes, and there's a note!" George cheered. "Papa, is it from Santa?"

"It is, my boy. It says 'Dear Everett Family, it's Santa. I hope you're having a very Merry Christmas. I'm leaving this note with these gifts to tell you a little secret. They're not from me.

That's right. They're from someone very special, who loves you very much. You know that I have helper elves. But did you know that you have your own helper elf too? His name is Sniff, and he is a house-elf. He lives with you, though you can't see him. He's the one who did all of this for you. The decorations and nutcrackers, and these presents. He did it to show you all how much he loves you. He's probably there with you right now! Under your feet or maybe in the walls. I just thought you'd like to know that there is someone else in your family, hoping to help you however he can. Merry Christmas! From Santa Claus and Sniff the House Elf.' Well, how about that?"

"We have our own helper elf? Amazing." Molly and George said together.

"That'd explain a lot, wouldn't it dear?"

"Sure does! Well, wherever you are... Thank you, Sniff!"

And that's the story of how a Christmas elf and a house-elf worked together to make a very special Christmas for one lovely family. So, the next time you find a lost sock or your favorite locket, or come home to your house looking extra clean, be sure to thank your house elf. Because we are there all year round, and we love you. You Big

Folk make every day Christmas for us. Thank you.

Sincerely,

Sniff the House Elf

THE END

Chapter 3: The Sleigh Ride

One Christmas Eve, I went out on a sleigh ride. It was a very ordinary sleigh, on a very ordinary Christmas. As ordinary as Christmas can be, at least. The sun had gone down, and the lamps were all lit. The snow was falling softly on my hat, and I had to shake it a couple of times. It made the orange glow of the lamps look magical orbs, dancing as I rode past. My nose started to get red in the cold wind, but I didn't mind. I liked to watch my breath drift away in clouds through the night sky.

My horses, Cupid and Vixen, had long shaggy hair. The snowflakes would get caught in their mane, like little bits of winter magic. Their breaths made even bigger clouds than mine, and the lamplight made everything glow in this magical way. The streets and cobblestone shimmered under the snow. The snowflakes sparkled, like bits of crystal drifting in the wind. It was a perfect Christmas Eve.

On the side of the road, people were out caroling. The traditional songs filled the night air. "Jingle Bells" and "Hark, Hear the Bells," all the classics. My town was small, so we don't get many carolers at Christmas. Just a handful of people who do it every year. And that's when I had a great idea. I pulled my sleigh over and looked down at the cold carolers. They looked up at me, holding their candles in shivering hands. They wore old-timey clothes, like cloaks and capes, but that didn't look to be helping them much in the cold.

"Merry Christmas, Carolers. I've got an idea you might like. How about we spread your songs all around town."

"What do you mean?" One lady asked me.

"Let's make Jingle Bells come true. We'll ride around in my sleigh, and you can sing carols for the whole town!"

The snow started to fall harder, gathering on the brim of my top hat. The whisper of wind filled our ear.

"I don't think it's a bad idea. We'll get to sing for everyone this way." One caroler said.

"Yeah! And it's Christmas. Who doesn't want to sing and ride in a sleigh on Christmas?"

And so, everyone climbed into the back of my sleigh. It wasn't very big, but it was enough to hold six people at least. Cupid and Vixen didn't seem to mind. They were big horses, more than enough to pull a whole wagon. And when I shook the reigns, the carolers began to sing a beautiful song.

"O holy night the stars are brightly shining

It is the night of our dear Savior's birth

Long lay the world in sin and error pining

Till He appeared, and the soul felt its worth

A thrill of hope the weary world rejoices

For yonder breaks a new glorious morn

Fall on your knees

O hear the angels' voices

O night divine

O night when Christ was born

O night divine o night

O night divine

A thrill of hope the weary world rejoices

For yonder breaks a new glorious morn

Fall on your knees

O hear the angels' voices

O night divine

O night when Christ was born

O night divine o night

O night divine

Ooh yes it was

Ooh it is the night of our dear Savior's birth

Oh yeah, oh yeah, oh yeah, yeah

It was a holy holy holy, oh oh oh"

"We're closed! It's Christmas. Come back tomorrow, kid." An old man shouted at me, appearing from behind the door.

"Please, sir. I need to buy a gift for my big brother. Anything. I have fifty cents. What can that get me?"

"A toy from that machine. Goodnight, kid. Merry Christmas."

The old man shut off the lights, and I was left standing under a night sky, all alone, with no idea of what to do next. I slumped against an old toy machine and looked at the stars. There was no snow, and I could barely see the sky through the city lights. But the first star, the brightest star of the night, came out. All I could do now was wish.

"Oh, Christmas Star. Please, hear me. I need your help. I want to get my brother something he really wants. No, something he needs. He's always been there for me, but I can't help him. If only there was someone who he could rely on too."

Suddenly the machine I was leaning on started humming and buzzing, making me jump.

Turning around, I realized it was glowing. The lights on it were green and red. Christmas themed. On the front were all these cartoon characters, posing and saying things in Japanese.

"Brother likes to watch shows like these. If I can't get him anything else, maybe I can get him a toy. I hope he likes it."

I put my fifty cents into the coin slot and turned the nob. Cranking it once, twice, three times, I wondered what type of present Brother would get. And then the machine started shaking back and forth. Lights glowed even brighter, green and red sparks started to shoot out. Christmas music started to play. "Rockin' Around the Christmas Tree," I think. The lights and sparks got so bright, like a Christmas themed firework. Thinking the machine was going to explode, I backed away and closed my eyes.

And then it stopped.

"Uh, excuse me? Little Girl? Can you tell me what day it is?"

I opened my eyes, confused. It looked like the lights and music, and even the sparks had all stopped. The machine had gotten quiet and standing in front of it was a pretty lady with bright purple hair. She looked like she was Japanese and even had an accent.

"Yeah... sure... It's Christmas Eve."

"Christmas Eve? Oh boy! My first Christmas Eve! What a great first day. What are the chances that I'd get picked on Christmas?"

"Picked? What do you mean, lady?"

"I don't really know, Bee! All I know is that it's Christmas, and your brother is probably worried sick. Come on, let's go home."

The lady was dressed in some sort of robe, with pretty flowers on it. White and red, just like Santa! I didn't say that though. I didn't say anything. I just stared at her and wondered where she came from. And then she took my hand, smiling at me. She was so pretty!

"My name is Sakura. I'm here to help you and your brother. Come on."

Sakura and I rode the cable car back to the house. When we got home, Brother was sitting on the stairs. Probably waiting for me.

"Oh no..."

"What's wrong, Bee?"

"My big brother... He's probably angry."

"I don't think so. Your brother loves you very much." Sakura said, petting my head softly.

"How do you know?"

"I'm not sure. I just do."

"Bee?! Bee! Thank God. Bee, are you okay?" Before I realized it, Brother was picking me up off the ground and spinning me around. His arms squeezed me tight. "Where were you? I was so worried! I thought you got lost. I was going to call the cops. Never mind that. Are you okay?"

"Yeah, I'm okay. I just wanted to get you a Christmas gift. But nobody would take my fifty cents... And then-"

"And then she found me," Sakura said softly, standing at the bottom of the steps.

"Oh. Hi. You found my sister? I really owe you one. Thank you so much, Miss-"

"Sakura. My name is Sakura."

"Big brother. Sakura doesn't have any family, or friends, or anywhere to go for Christmas. Can she stay here?"

"I don't know, Bee. We don't have much space..."

"Please, brother! She's my pre-"

"I don't want to be any trouble," Sakura said, turning to walk away.

"Wait. Miss Sakura? It's okay. You can stay in my room. I'll take the couch. Why don't you come upstairs? You too, Bee." My brother put me down on the steps, and he held the door open for both of us.

"Thank you," Sakura said, smiling at my brother and tucking her purple hair back.

In the distance, someone started singing Christmas carols. We all went upstairs into the warm and shared a big dinner. Brother made ham, pie, and even pudding. Between the three of us, we ate it all. Which was nice, because we always have leftovers. After that, we sat around the living room and watched old Christmas movies. Sakura changed into a pair of my brother's pajamas, even though they were too big for her. During the Polar Express, Brother fell asleep on the couch. He snored loudly, and I started to tease him. But then I saw something that made me smile. Sakura was sleeping on the couch too, laying on top of my brother. And they were snoring together.

I love Christmas with my brother. I wouldn't trade it for anything in the world. Sometimes I miss Mom and Dad, and the big Christmas parties we'd have. And sometimes it got a little lonely. It was just Brother and me, after all. But for the first time in a long time, I felt like I had a whole family. Sakura was a part of the family. And we were happy. I fell asleep wondering if Brother and Sakura would get married. Maybe they'd even get married on a Christmas like today.

And that's the story of how I gave my brother the Christmas gift of Love.

THE END

Chapter 5: The Christmas Forest

You can find magic anywhere. Especially during Christmas. That's the time of year where Christmas is everywhere. Written in the stars, dancing on the moon, swinging through the trees, and even in your own home. During Christmas time, you should look for magic wherever you can. Under the bed, in your shoes, and especially in your backyard. Because that's where I found it. Magic! Real magic.

It was Christmas Day. My whole family was at the house, exchanging gifts and talking about what nice toys they got. It was super warm inside my little home, and the fire was crackling. The whole living room smelled like ham, and cinnamon, and cookies. It was nice and cozy, but I didn't want to be inside. Not on Christmas Day. And that's because it was snowing out!

I asked all my brothers, sisters, and cousins if they wanted to go outside. But nobody listened. There was too much shouting and laughing, and banging of toys. They only cared about their presents. But I wanted to play in the snow. So, I went to the door, and I pulled on my socks. And then I pulled on the second pair of socks. I put on my boots. They were really tight and really warm, with two pairs of socks on.

I wrapped my face up in a fuzzy scarf that made my nose itch and pulled on my gloves. They had big red snowflakes on them, they're my favorite pair. And then I pulled my jacket on over my red-and-green Christmas sweater. Nobody looked at me. They were too busy eating some tasty ham and laughing at what was on TV. So, I got ready and opened the big wooden door that led to my backyard. A blast of snow hit me square in the face, and a cold wind pushed me back. But that wasn't going to stop me. I took my first steps into the Christmas blizzard.

biggest bird in all the wood. I need your help, Miss Owl."

"Oho! Well, doesn't everyone! Pretty words can only get you so far, Silly Child. What do you need?"

"Nothing much. Nothing that the Great Miss Owl can't do. It's just that I'm lost, Miss Owl. I followed Mister Fox into the woods. We were playing a game. But I lost my way. I couldn't tell which way my home was. I don't know which way is forward and which way is back. And then, in a circle of red pine trees, I met Miss Squirrel. I asked her for help, but she was too busy collecting acorns for her family. And so, she told me to climb into this log. And while crawling through the log, I met Mama Ladybug and her family. They told me that you were just the animal I needed. That you're the smartest, and that you'd know just how to help me. And then I met Mister Butterfly here-"

"Hello." Mister Butterfly says ever-so-quietly.

"And here we are. So, what do you think, Miss Owl? Can you help me? Will you help me? Please, I just want to find my way back home."

The wind was cold as it danced around the nest, and snow slowly moved around our feet, like the current of a pale river. I shivered, Mister Butterfly closed his wings tight, and Miss Owl began to sway with the breeze. Almost like she was a part of the tree too!

"Hmmm. Hmmmmmm." She hummed softly, closing her eyes. Maybe she was thinking to herself? "Hmmm. Everyone wants something. Every blade of grass needs the sun, every bee needs the flowers, and every bird needs the wind. Everyone needs something, but nobody asks what I need."

"What do you need, Miss Owl?"

The big bird opened one of her bright amber eyes and stared at me. A few flakes of snow settled on her golden beak, then fell off when she started to speak again.

"What do I need? What do I need? Peace! Quiet! Everyone is always coming to me for something."

"Isn't that what happens when you are the wisest bird in all the forest? We need your help. And only you can help us." Mister Butterfly said suddenly.

"Wrong! Wrong, Mister Butterfly. I can't help you. Now that the child has come into our wood, only one can help. It is the magic of today. Only one can lead the Silly Child out of the forest and to their home. The only one who can go between our world and theirs is the Guardian."

"But we don't know where the Guardian is. Only the Wisest or the Bravest know where the Guardian is." Mister Butterfly says back, shocked.

I didn't know what they were talking about. Worlds? I knew about magic, sure. But who is the Guardian? And that's what I asked.

"Who is the Guardian? Miss Owl, Mister Butterfly?"

"Oh, Silly Child." Mister Butterfly said in his gentle voice. "You know so much, yet so little. The Guardian is the Guardian. There is no explanation. They simply guard what is sacred in this forest. The oldest trees, the cleanest rivers, the quiet caves. The places we animals love. The places that make the forest what it is. The Guardian is the oldest animal and the strongest. And only a few animals know them."

"Yes." Miss Owl said, nodding slowly. As if she knew something. "Only the Wisest, the Bravest, or the Swiftest know who the Guardian is. And where they are."

"And we don't know who the Wisest, or the Bravest, or the Swiftest are." Mister Butterfly says sadly. "I'm sorry, Silly Child. I can't help you."

"Wait..." I say, looking between the butterfly and the owl. "Miss Owl. Are you the Wisest?"

The feathers on the top of Miss Owl's head stand up, getting all fluffy. Her amber eyes narrow. "What? What makes you say that, Silly Child?"

"I just know. I don't know why. But it's you, isn't it? I'm right, aren't I? You're the Wisest!"

"Oh! Oh. Maybe you aren't so silly after all, Silly Child. Maybe I was wrong about you..."

"What?" Mister Butterfly says softly. "Miss Owl, are you saying you really are the Wisest?"

"I am!"

"She is!" I shout, happiness filling my heart. I felt hope again.

"Does that mean..."

"Yes, Mister Butterfly. I know who the Guardian is. But I have not seen them in a long time."

"Oh no! Miss Owl, does this mean you really can't help?"

"Wrong, Silly Child! I can help. I can bring you to the Swiftest. They may know where the Guardian is! They were the last one to see them, after all."

"But where is the Swiftest, Miss Owl?" Mister Butterfly asks, leaving my shoulder and flying in circles around my head. In the sunlight, his violet wings were glowing and beautiful.

Miss Owl points a white feather towards the big mountains in the distance and hoots loudly. "The Swiftest likes to live on the edge of the forest, at the bottom of the Sleeping Serpent Mountains."

I gasped, looking at the mountains and then Miss Owl. "In the Appalachians? Oh no! I'll never make it there and back before dinner. My family is going to be so angry with me."

"The Silly Child is right, Miss Owl. It will take days for their little legs to carry them all the way to the Sleeping Serpent Mountains. Isn't there another way?"

"Oh, there is. But I'm so tired. And I don't feel like flying in a blizzard."

I took a step forward, raising my hands in a plea. I did my very best to give the puppy dog eyes Mom was always talking about, but I don't know if I did it very well. "Please, Miss Owl. You're the only hope I've got. You've already helped so much. But if you can help me one more time, I'll love you forever."

"A Silly Child's love? Hmph! Alright alright, just stop with the eyes. I'll help you. But only because you're asking so nicely. Just wait here."

"Wait here? Okay, if you say so."

Miss Owl stood up from her nest then, and I was amazed. She was even bigger when she was standing. Taller than I was! And when she spread her wings and began to flap them, she created a wind almost as strong as the blizzard! Loose feathers and pieces of wood flew out of the nest as Miss Owl rose into the air and dove off the nest.

"Nicely done, you Silly Child. Very few people get Ol' Lady Owl's help with anything. She isn't the helping type. She prefers to sleep, eat, and be alone. That's why she's up here, in this nest. I think she likes talking to the clouds and the stars." Mister Butterfly said to me after Miss Owl had gone.

"I think she is very nice. And the stars and clouds have a lot to talk about. Maybe that's why she is so wise!"

"Spoken like a truly Silly Child. Maybe you're right, though." He whispered, before landing on my head again.

"I think we should all spend less time listening to what others say about us, and more time listening to what the stars have to tell us. They're older and wiser than we will ever be."

"You're smarter than you look, Silly Child."

"Thank you, Mister Butterfly."

And then a massive gust of wind pushed me down into the nest. Thank goodness I was wearing a warm hat, or my hair would have been flying everywhere, and I would have been freezing! And then, I heard something different. *Whoosh, whoosh, whoosh.* The distinct sound of wings flapping, but bigger. Louder. And then the white and gold head of Ol' Lady Owl appeared over the edge of the nest. But bigger now. Much bigger. She was the size of a horse! Her feathers had gotten longer and shinier too. She hovered there in the air, glowing gold and pushing us back with all the wind her wings made.

"Well? Are you going to just sit there, Silly Child? I won't wait here all day. Get on my back already."

"You're back? Miss Owl, what happened to you? How did you get so big?"

"Oh, never mind that, will you? You've got more important things to be doing right now. Like flying across a forest to find the Swiftest. You want to get home to your warm food, don't you? I'm sure you miss your nest, and I'm starting to miss mine already."

"Oh, okay!" I rose from the woven branches that made the giant nest and walked hesitantly to the edge.

"So how do I..."

"Just jump, child! I'll catch you on my back."

"Are you sure? We're so high up. I don't want to fa-"

"Are you saying you don't trust me? The Wisest? If you want to walk instead, you can just slide back down the dead log and-"

"No! We want your help. I'll jump." I stood on the edge of the nest, looking down at the tops of the trees below. I had to be at least one hundred feet in the air. Maybe even two hundred! The tall pine trees looked like tiny sticks from way up here. Looking up, it was like I could almost touch the clouds. And even though the wind and snow were icy cold, my heart started to race, and my palms broke out in a sweat. A small part of me wanted to climb back into the nest and just stay there forever. But another side of me knew that this was important. I needed to be brave. To make this leap. So that I could get back home. If I didn't, I would just regret it later. After all, it isn't every day that someone gets to ride on the back of a giant owl in a snowstorm.

"Go on, Silly Child. You can do it. You need to do it." Mister Butterfly encouraged, before flying over and landing on Miss Owl. "I'll wait right here for you."

And that's when I jumped. The wind burned my eyes but stole the tears away. My scarf flapped wildly, tugging this way and that. Even my sweat was blown away by the cold air as I fell. And then, just as quickly as I had been falling, I wasn't. I was flying. The impact of landing on Miss Owl's back was like landing in a bed of feathers. Probably because she was covered in them.

"Silly Child! I didn't think you'd jump without telling me first."

"Oh. I'm sorry. I just needed to do it. Just take the first step. No hesitation, no doubt."

"Bravery isn't having no fear. Bravery is looking at the face of fear and not giving it a chance to stop you." Mister Butterfly says softly, landing on the back of my hand.

My hands buried into the white feathers, holding tight. I didn't want to fall, but I didn't want to hurt Miss Owl either. The winds were strong. The snow never stopped, and we flew straight into the blizzard. I pulled my scarf closer to my face, covering my frozen nose. But that only made me colder. When I touched my scarf again, I realized it had turned to ice. And when I ran my hand along Miss Owl's back, I felt her feathers starting to freeze too. I realize how difficult it must be to fly through a snowstorm. Or at least, how unpleasant. Looking up at the sky, I saw a sea of grey, with a patch of sunlight here or there. Looking down, I saw a sea of emerald swaying with the wild winds. Pine trees bending to the storm.

"Miss Owl, thank you so much. I know it's cold, and probably hard to fly in this weather."

"Oh, please! This is nothing for me. I am the Wisest, and the greatest bird in the whole forest, remember? I've flown through storms much bigger."

"I know. But still. Thank you. It's only polite to show love to someone who helps you." I rub my hand along the back of the gold and white feathers, pushing the snow and ice away. I was trying my best to help somehow.

"You know, you really are a silly child." Mister Butterfly said.

"I know." Closing my eyes, I felt Miss Owl sail along the currents of the storm. The icy winds climbed inside of me and danced, then left just as quick. I'd never flown before. Never been in a plane. And here I was, on Christmas Day, riding a giant owl through a blizzard. Not what I expected when I went outside to play in the snow.

Miss Owl's voice drifted up to me and pulled me from daydreaming. "Silly Child! We're almost to the den of the Swiftest. I hope that you know what you're going to say!"

"What do you mean, Miss Owl? You aren't going to stay with us and speak with the Swiftest too?"

"Me? What? Are you crazy? No way, no how. I'm not staying out in this cold, you Silly Child. I'm going to go back to my nice, cozy nest." Then without even a head's up, Miss Owl dove down towards the base of the mountains. "I'm going to go back and sleep right through this awful blizzard. Sleep until I can't sleep anymore."

We started to fly in circles, down towards the ground. Beside us, the Appalachian Mountains were tall and mysterious. Covered in a thick layer of snow, they were more white than green, and some thick grey clouds were floating around near the top. I loved staring at the mountains. They made me feel safe and comfortable. Probably because I had been looking at them my whole life. Below us was a small grove with peculiar trees. They had silver bark and bright red leaves. They stood out against the snow like red paint against a canvas. So bright, so inviting. A safe place that would shelter you from the blizzards and snow.

"Is that the den of the Swiftest, Miss Owl?"

"What's that? Oh. Sharp eyes! Yeah, that's it. The Spring Grove, we call it. You'll see why."

As we landed outside the Spring Grove, I gasped. The trees were even more beautiful in person. The bark didn't just look silver; it was silver! Light bounced off the wood, making the whole tree look as if it was glowing. And the light that reflected off the bark shone into the leaves above, making them glow an even brighter red. Almost like someone was taking a flashlight and shining it through them. Mister Butterfly and I got off Miss Owl's back. I thought I would land in a bunch of snow, but the ground was completely dry. Just a layer of deep green grass and a few dry leaves floating around.

"Well, this is as far as I take you. The Swiftest is inside the Spring Grove. You tell 'em I say hello. I'd love to stick around, but the blizzards still going up there." Shaking the snow from her feathered body, Ol' Lady Owl blinks at us with her big amber eyes. "It was nice meeting you, Silly Child. Remember me next time you hear an owl hoot. And try not to get lost again, would you?"

"I will, Miss Owl. It was nice to meet you too! Stay warm and fly safely."

"Yes, don't get lost in all that snow." Mister Butterfly adds to the farewell, fluttering around my head again.

"Oh, I won't. I'm the Wisest, remember? Enjoy the warm weather while you can!" And with a few flaps of her golden wings, she was gone. Off into the blizzard again.

I didn't realize it until then. The weather was completely different there. Sure, there was no snow on the ground, but it was more than that. The snow wasn't falling there at all. The blizzard had completely disappeared, and the sun was even out! It was warm enough that the snow had already melted off my clothes, and Mister Butterfly was floating towards a nearby flower. I wondered what made this part of the forest different than the rest. Why it was so hot too! I was starting to sweat in my coat. It reminded me of the log tunnel I had to climb through to reach Ol' Lady Owl's nest. Flowers were growing there too. And just like in the log, there were other friendly insects and moss everywhere.

"It's the trees." Mister Butterfly said as he flew back towards me.

"What?" I asked, breaking out of my wonder.

"The weather. You're wondering why it is different here, right? Why the weather is warmer, and there are so many flowers? "

"Oh. Yes, I was."

"Well, it's the trees. The silver bark of the trees catches the light, and that light bounces off warms the field and grove. When the light reaches the leaves, they hold onto the light and warmth even longer. At night, when the sun goes down, the leaves still glow read from all the light they have inside them. It makes the whole area warmer and stops the cold. The sunlight in the silver bark and leaves melts the snow before it can get close and feeds the plants and grass around us."

"And that's why you call it the Spring Grove?"

"Yes, Silly Child. That's why we call it the Spring Grove. Well, one of the reasons. There's also the inside." Mister Butterfly said, his wings fluttering as he flies in circles around me.

Before I could say anything else, a strong wind pushed at my back, shoving me forward. I caught myself, after almost falling into a beautiful little bunch of lily-of-the-valley but looked around confused. This wind was different. It wasn't the blizzard winds I felt while flying with Miss Owl, which was cold as the north pole and left my scarf covered in ice. This gust was more like a spring breeze, moving my hair and cooling the sweat on my forehead. It smelled like flowers that had just bloomed, and wet dirt, and grass that was

81

pushing out of the soil. It smelled like wood that had been sitting in the sunlight for a long time and tree pollen. It smelled like the warm season.

"Well, are you coming in? Or are you just going to stand outside and keep me waiting?" A voice called from behind the silver trees. As it spoke, the red leaves danced in the wind. As if the wind and the voice were connected in some way.

"That's the Swiftest. It must be. Come, let's not keep them waiting."

"What do you think the Swiftest looks like, Mister Butterfly?"

"No point in focusing on what maybe when you can move forward and find the answers. They're right in front of you."

"You're right. Let's go!"

I slipped through the wall of silver trees, running my hand along the glowing bark as I went. It was warm, like a stone that had been left out in the sun. And smooth, almost like the marble counters in my mom's kitchen. I stepped around small bushes of wild berries and monkshood. I tried to be careful. 'Don't bother the plants.' I told myself. 'Because this is their home. How would I want someone to treat me or my home?' If some stranger came walking into my garden, I hope they'd show me the same kindness.

Tiptoeing around the flowers and bushes and walking between the silver trees with their red leaves, I realized that this grove was a lot bigger than it looked from the sky. I had been walking through the glowing trees for a few minutes now, and I still couldn't see the center. After a few more minutes of wandering, I began to wonder if I was going the wrong way.

"No, you're going the right way." Mister Butterfly told me. "It isn't the direction you're going; it's the way you're thinking. Do you remember when you were running on top of the snow? You had to think light thoughts. And when you wanted to go up the dead log? You had to think of up thoughts. This place is the same. So, all you need to do to reach the Grove of Spring is think of-"

"Spring! Right! Of course. You're so smart, Mister Butterfly. Where would I be without you?"

"Oh, you'd be fine, you Silly Child. You'd just take a little longer to figure it out. But we all need a little help sometimes."

So, I closed my eyes and filled my mind with spring. What did spring smell like? Fresh dew on flower petals. Trees budding and growing new leaves. Rain showers on hot dirt. What did spring sound like? Swallows and blue jays and robins, singing outside the window. Baby birds, chirping away as they break out of their shells. The buzz of bumblebees dancing between flowers. The soft tapping of a sun shower on the rocks outside. What does spring look like? Baby bunnies, hopping through the bright green grass. Blues and purples, reds and oranges, popping up from the ground in the form of new butterflies. The river by the house, gurgling and flowing again, babbling happily. Butterflies fluttering in the breeze. What does spring feel like? Warm sunshine kissing me as I finally wear a t-shirt again. Grass, soft and cool under my bare feet. Shade from the new leaves on the tree offering me comfort on the very hot days. A gentle breeze with the smell of flowers passing over me as I lay in the grass.

And just as I thought of that breeze, one came dancing through the trees, making the branches whisper to each other noisily. It tugged on my jacket and pushed me forward. And when I opened my eyes, I was looking at a giant grove!

Or was it a meadow? Or both! Fields of flowers, just like the ones I imagined, spread out in front of me. Monkshood and lily-of-the-valley, milkwort and cardinal flower, milkweed, and azaleas! All my favorite flowers, the ones that made spring special, dancing in the warm breeze. A small brook cut through the center, sparkling in the sunshine. It laughed and giggled as it passed over pale white rocks. I followed the creek, watching the small fish and frogs that were living inside. A few croaked at me as I went past.

I stepped through the field of flowers slowly, taking in this new weather. Winter winds and soft snow is always nice, but after a couple of hours of being outside, you get tired. The feeling of soft petals touching my hands as I walked past, the sun hugging me and warming my insides; they were refreshing. I stopped for a moment by the creek, getting down on my knees. I didn't mind the dirt or the way the frogs looked at me like I was crazy.

"What are you doing, Silly Child? Don't you want to get home?"

"Of course, I do, Mister Butterfly! But I also want to enjoy this moment. The weather is beautiful. And I bet this water feels really nice."

"Oh, it is." One frog croaked at me, hopping on over to rest by my knee. She was a happy little frog, with brown spots on her back. The other frogs looked at me like they were scared, but this one was friendly. And when she looked up at me, she even smiled. "Why don't you try it out? I bet you'll like it so much you'll take a swim."

"I wish I could take a swim, Little Frog. But I'm just too big. Thanks for the offer, though." I tugged my gloves off and dipped my hands in the water. The crystal-clear liquid flowed around my fingers as if they weren't there, but I felt it. The water was gentle and cool, but not cold. Suddenly I wanted to just sit there and dip my feet in. Forget about my home. Forget about my worries.

"Maybe I could just stay here, living in this meadow without a care in the world. I'm sure Mom and Dad will be fine without me. They have my sisters. And this place is just so nice. So quiet and peaceful. Not like when my family comes over."

"You say that now, but you love your family. It is easy to take for granted what's always there. But if they weren't around, you'd want them to be. You'd miss them." The Little Frog croaked.

"Yeah, you're right. But I don't want to leave this place. Can I come back to it one day?"

Mister Butterfly landed on a white flower that sat by the creek and watched the water flow. "Life is like this brook. No matter what, it keeps on flowing. You can look behind you and remember the twists and turns, and you can look in front of you to see where it bends, but you can only see so far. And no matter what is behind you or in front of you, the creek will still carry you forward. Sometimes you're better off just letting it flow."

"I think what Mister Butterfly is trying to say is we don't know if you'll come back here or not. The best you can do is keep following the creek and hope that it will lead you back one day." The Little Frog told me as she looked at the water with her big eyes.

"I guess you're both right. I just like this place a lot."

I leaned back into the grass and flowers, folding my arms behind my head. The clouds were little puffs of white overhead. They drifted so slowly.

Not like the big, fast-moving clouds of the blizzard. Those were like giant ships, sailing through the sky. But these were like little white canoes, floating along at peace. I was starting to float away with them. The day had been so long, and I was starting to get sleepy. And just when I was ready to let my eyes shut, something moved beside me. I heard the snap of a twig and a slurp of water, so I turned my head to see what it was. And that's when I saw it. The Swiftest. Or at least, I'm pretty sure he was the Swiftest.

"Why are you staring, Silly Child?"

"Oh, I'm sorry. I don't mean to stare." I didn't move or sit up. Part of me didn't want to. The wind had such a soothing touch, and the sight of the blue sky had calmed me. But this creature beside me was beautiful. He had the body of a mountain lion and the tail of a fox. His head was long and narrow like a wolf, but it had a rack of bright silver antlers on its head.

"You act as you've never seen a blue wildebeest before." He said to me as he lowered his shaggy head back down to drink some more.

It was true. I'd never seen a blue wildebeest before. I'd never seen a wildebeest period. I wasn't sure what a wildebeest was. Was it a cat? A dog? Something in between? And so, I climbed off the bank of the creek and sat facing the wildebeest as he drank. His fur was the same color as the water he drank. A blue so bright that he might have been a piece of the sky above us that fell and became a beast.

"Well, you're right. I haven't. I haven't seen a wildebeest, blue or red or yellow or purple. What is a wildebeest, Mister Wildebeest."

"Please, just Wildebeest." The large creature sat back on his paws, giving me a funny look. "A wildebeest is a wildebeest. Nothing more to it. We just are what we are. Like everyone else. We might look like one thing or another, but we aren't anything other than wildebeests. There aren't many of us these days, though. I might even be the last wildebeest."

"Are you magic?"

"Aren't you?" He asks me, smiling a fanged smile.

"Am I? I don't think so. If I was magic, I'd just poof my way home."

"Everyone and everything in the world is magic. And no magic is the same. Your magic isn't my magic. My magic isn't your magic."

"Excuse me." Mister butterfly flaps on over to land on the grass between Wildebeest and I. His purple wings glowed in the sunlight. "Are you the Swiftest, sir?"

"Hello, Mister Butterfly." Wildebeest leaned down low to look at the little butterfly sitting in front of him. His silver nose glowed, just like Mister Butterfly's wings.

'They're the same silver as the trees.' I thought to myself, sitting quietly.

"Yes, I am the Swiftest. The one who runs the forest. But why do you ask?"

"It is the Silly Child. They need your help."

Wildebeest lifted his shaggy blue head and looked at me. "Is that true? You need help?"

"Yes, Wildebeest. I need help. I need to leave the forest, you see. I left my home to come play in the snow, and that's when I met Mister Fox. He invited me to a game of tag, and I thought that was a great idea. So, I chased Mister Fox through the snow and into this forest. But then I lost him in a grove of red pine trees. When I looked around, I didn't know where I was. And that was when I met Miss Squirrel. She was very nice, and I asked her to help me get back home, but she was too busy gathering acorns for her family. But then she pointed me to a dead log, where I would find the animal who could help me. It was in the log that I met Mister Butterfly here."

"Hello again." Mister Butterfly said softly, fluttering his wings.

"And then, when I got to the top of the dead log, I was in Miss Owl's nest. Did you know she lives above the whole forest? In the tallest tree, I think."

"I did know. But she doesn't live in the tallest tree. She lives in the second tallest tree."

"Oh really? Where is the tallest tree, Wildebeest? What does it look like?"

"That doesn't matter, Silly Child. Tell your story."

"Oh okay. Well, it's almost done. When we met with Miss Owl, she told us that only the Guardian could help me get out of the forest. But only the Wisest, the Swiftest, and the Bravest know where the Guardian is."

"Isn't Miss Owl the Wisest though?" Wildebeest asked, raising his fuzzy eyebrows.

"She sure is! But she didn't know where the Guardian is. But that's why she flew us here. She told us that the Swiftest might know where the Guardian is! So, do you?"

"I don't."

"You don't?" Mister Butterfly asked, landing on his flower again.

"I don't. I don't know where the Guardian is. I only know that the Bravest was the last one to speak with the Guardian."

"That's not good. That's not good at all. This Silly Child needs to-"

"No, don't worry, Mister Butterfly. It's fine. It'll all be okay."

"You aren't worried?" Wildebeest asked me, his bright eyes turning to me.

"Nope. Should I be? Things have been working out just fine so far. I'll find my way home. I just know it."

"I like that attitude, you Silly Child. You're right, you will find your way home. But I'm going to help you. Let me take you to see the Bravest. They will help you find the Guardian, I'm sure."

"You will? Really? Oh, thank you, Wildebeest!" I stood up and hugged his blue, fuzzy neck with all my strength. The claws and fangs and antlers didn't scare me. This was a friend. I could just tell. When I let go, Wildebeest was smiling at me.

"You're welcome. Come on, climb on my back. It'd take too long to walk there. We'll run."

"Couldn't I just run next to you?"

"You really are a Silly Child. They call me the Swiftest for a reason. Come on." Wildebeest got down low, giving me the chance to climb on his back. That's when I realized how big he was. Way bigger than a wolf. Maybe even bigger than a mountain lion. But he was soft, like my dog at home. I did my best to climb up, then I wrapped my arms around his neck.

"Is this okay? I'm not hurting you, right?"

"Yes, Silly Child. I'm okay. Just hold on tight. Are you ready?"

"Yeah! Let's go!"

"Are you ready, Mister Butterfly."

My little purple friend had settled down between Wildebeest's antlers, closing his wings tight. "Yes, I'm ready. Let's go."

It felt like we were flying all over again. Not because we were so high up, but because of how strong the wind was. One moment we were in the grove, with birds chirping around us. The next moment, the wind was rushing past my ears in a muted roar. My scarf chased behind me, flapping about, and the loose strands of my hair followed it. I couldn't see anything at all. We were moving that fast. I did notice the blurs suddenly go from bright colors like purple and red to green and white. Which means we left the Spring Grove and the silver trees behind. Part of me was very sad about that. And another part of me hoped I'd go back someday and get to talk with the nice frog and watch the clouds overhead. I'd lay back and let my feet soak in the cool brook and fall asleep beneath the open sky.

That trip was much shorter than the flight with Miss Owl though. It must have been why they called him the Swiftest. Going so fast that the world was just a blur. Running through trees, and across frozen streams. I think we even sped over a frozen lake at one point. I wasn't sure. All I really knew was that the whole thing was over before I knew it. And when the world stopped spinning, we were standing in front of a giant hill, covered in moss and snow. The pine trees stopped some of the blizzard's wind, but not all of it. And in the falling streams of snow, the cave looked very cozy.

I climbed Wildebeest's back and hopped down into the snow. The Spring Grove was beautiful and comforting, I admit. A warm break from the constant blizzard winds and snow in my boots. But I missed the winter wonderland of the forest. The drifting snow that looked like fairy dust as it was picked up in the patches of sunlight. The banks of cold, which looked like small mountain ranges just waiting to be explored. The way everything glowed when the sunlight hit it just right, making the magic jump out at you. There's nothing like the sight of the winter wonderland to make your heart sing and light up a fire in your heart. There is something pure and innocent in the snow that makes you feel free. Like you're one of the snowflakes floating on along in the cold air.

"This is the cave of the Bravest. She is sleeping right now, but we can wake her together. I don't want her getting the wrong idea. But if she sees we are together, she won't be so grumpy."

"Grumpy? I don't want to bother her, Wildebeest. If she is sleeping, maybe we should come back in a little while? When she wakes up?"

"She won't wake up again until the snow begins to melt, and winter is behind us. This is her way, her season of rest."

Mister Butterfly landed on the top of my head and said, "It is what it is. You need her help. And that means it can't be helped."

"That's right." Wildebeest agreed, nodding his shaggy head, shaking the snow from his blue fur. "If you want to find the Guardian, you need her help."

"Are you sure she will help us? Even if we woke her up?"

"Like I said, that's why I'm here. We'll take it one step at a time, together."

And that was what we did. Literally. One step at a time, we pushed forward. One step at a time, we tiptoed through the snow. We had to wake her, but we weren't going to be rude about it. I was following the Wildebeest's trail. He went first, putting one paw in front of the other, gently walking across the top of the snow. He seemed familiar with the cave, and this area. And he seemed wise, just like Mister Butterfly. Maybe not as wise as Miss Owl, the Wisest, but still smart. So, I had to trust them. Trust that they knew what was best. As we walked into the cave, the snow disappeared from the ground. What we were walking on was just as soft though, even if it wasn't the white blanket of winter. The light disappeared briefly, but that didn't last long. Going from the bright snowy forest outside to the darkness in the cave, it didn't surprise me. And my eyes adjusted quickly, picking up little hints of light here and there. They were deep in the cave. It was a different kind of light. Not sunlight, but a soft glow. And the lights were the same color as Wildebeest's fur.

"What is that, Wildebeest? That light?"

"Yes, I see it too." Mister Butterfly says, whispering in the quiet.

"Just give it a moment. You'll see."

We walked deeper into the cave, following Wildebeest shining form. As we went further, I realized that this cave was different. It wasn't cold and damp, but warm and humid. Like there was heat coming from the ground and the walls, or an invisible fire of some kind. And after a few moments, I could see everything. The light, the small blue orbs that danced through the warm cave, were fireflies. Blue fireflies. They were everywhere, flying through the air in rivers of light. They followed each other, swirling and seething like a cloud of a thousand tiny flames. They drifted about like embers from a big bonfire, but there was none. Just the fireflies, floating all around us. And when I looked down at the ground, I saw why it was so soft and warm. Instead of stone, the ground was covered in a deep blue moss. In my mind, I wondered if the moss and the fireflies were connected somehow. If the moss was blue because of the little glowing bugs, or if the bugs were blue because of the fuzzy moss.

"Wow. It's beautiful." I whispered, hearing my voice echo through the cave.

"Yes. The Bravest sure knows how to pick a cave. There aren't many like this in the world. And isn't it peaceful? I wouldn't mind napping through a season or two in here." Wildebeest nods, his foxlike tail swaying behind him.

"Yes, the moss looks like a very good bed. Would anyone care for a nap?" Mister Butterfly says, laughing softly.

"I think the child would rather nap in their bed, no?"

"Yeah, I guess so. So where is the Bravest, Wildebeest?"

"Oh, she's right over there. In the corner."

Looking at the corner, where a group of fireflies were floating in a circle overhead, I saw a big golden boulder. But as we moved closer, the boulder bigger, and fuzzier. I wondered if it was a different type of moss, but then the boulder moved. It puffed up, then let out a big snore. A snore so strong that it made my knees shake and the ground quake.

"What. Is. That?" Mister Butterfly asked, stunned by the sleeping beast. It was a bear!

"That. Is the Bravest. She's a lot nicer than she looks, I promise. We just need to figure out how to wake her up without making her mad."

"I thought you were going to do that, Wildebeest?" I asked, feeling a little nervous. I didn't want to wake up a beast this big.

"What? Me? Oh no. I'm here to make sure she doesn't think you're a rude human who just waltzed into her cave."

"This is going to well." Mister Butterfly whispered as he flew over to the sleeping beast.

"What should I do, Mister Butterfly?"

"Why not try a song, Silly Child? Everyone loves music. Though usually music is used to put beasts to sleep, maybe it can be used to wake them up too."

"But what song should I sing?"

"A song from the heart. Only a song from the heart will sound genuine to the Bravest as she sleeps."

"Sing about what your heart needs. And why you came." The Wildebeest says.

"About what my heart needs..."

What did my heart need? I couldn't decide what I wanted for dinner. I didn't know what my heart needed. But if I listened very carefully, I could hear my singing to me. So, I closed my eyes and listened. Hands clasped, eyes shut, cave silent. I let my heart tell me what it needed.

"Today is Christmas Day.

I left my home and family.

I just wanted to play, in snow and winter dreams.

But when I played too long.

I wandered too far, and my home was gone.

And now I've wandered here.

To a forest of magic, lights, no fear.

But today is Christmas Day.

And I miss my home and family.

Today is Christmas Day.

I want to go home, together we'll play.

My family and me.

My Christmas.

My Christmas.

My winter dreams."

I wasn't the best singer, but my mom always told me that a song from the heart was the most beautiful kind. And this song came straight from my heart. So, I did my best. I sang with all my heart. I sang with love and hope. And it worked! The Bravest started to wake up. She rolled over onto her back, showing off her big belly, which was as bright gold as the sun in the Spring Grove. And by the time my song was done, she had opened her eyes and let out a giant yawn.

"Who's singing while I'm trying to take a nap?" She growled sleepily and climbed off the bed of moss she had been napping on. Her big blue eyes were lowered to me, and I started to feel nervous. What if my song was wrong? What if I didn't sing well, or it wasn't pretty enough? "Don't you know you shouldn't poke a sleeping bear?" She asked me in a sleepy voice.

"Technically, the Silly Child sang for a sleeping bear." Mister Butterfly whispered, making a bad joke.

"It was me, Miss Bravest. I was the one singing for you. We needed to wake you up, and it was the best I could think of."

"Don't be mad, Miss Bear." Wildebeest said, stepping in front of us, his tail whipping back and forth. The Swiftest smiled at the Bravest and bowed its head. "I told them to wake you."

"Wildebeest? Why on earth would you tell them to wake me? You know I need my beauty sleep. Winter is my quiet season."

"I know, Miss Bear. I'm sorry to wake you up. And they are sorry too. But this child needs help. And you're the only one who can help them."

Miss Bear snorted, her breath coming out in two clouds of steam. She lowered her shimmering face down to me, and I tried to smile at her. Her head was bigger than I was, but that didn't scare me.

"Even though you're big and probably grumpy, you're not mean. I can tell."

"Oho? Is that so, you Silly Child? And how can you tell?"

"Your voice. I can tell from your voice, Miss Bear. You talk just like my mom. With a strong voice, but soft at the same time. It's a kind voice. Like a stone sitting out in the sun. You're tough, but warm too."

"Oho, are you sure? I could eat you up in one bite if I wanted." She smiled at me, showing off pointy golden teeth.

"You could," I told her. "But you won't. Because you don't want to. You just want to sleep."

"Oho, you really are a Silly Child! What about your song. Is that true? What you said about wanting to go home to your family? Do you miss them?"

"I do. I wanted to go out and play in the snow. But I think that was wrong. I should have stayed inside and played with them. Now I'm stuck out here, and I just wish I stayed and played with them while I could. I can always play in the snow tomorrow. But my family aren't all going to be together tomorrow. That's why Christmas is special. It's a time of year where everyone is together. It doesn't matter if we are all playing in the snow, or if we are all inside watching tv. All that matters is that we're together."

"You're right, Silly Child. It is better to be with family and warm in the den than outside and alone in the cold." Miss Bear said. She nodded and smiled at me, and that reminded me of my mom too. "My cubs were little like you once. But then they got big and decided to wander off on their own. They wanted to explore, climb mountains, and swim in rivers. And now they are as big as I am and have little cubs of their own. But they still come home once a year, during spring, to be with their Mama. Because they learned the same thing you have. Everything is better when the family is together."

"Does that mean you'll help me, Miss Bear?"

"Oho, call me Mama Bear."

"Okay! Mama Bear, will you please help me find the Guardian and go home?"

"Wildebeest, do you like this child?"

"Yes." The Wildebeest said, looking at me with glowing eyes. "I am quite fond of the Silly Child."

"Mister Butterfly? What do you think?"

"This one is different, Mama Bear. This one is alive with magic. And love." Mister Butterfly said as he flew around Mama Bear's big head.

"Oho, is that so? Alright, Silly Child. You have met the Wisest. She let you fly on her back and led you to the Swiftest. The Swiftest has met you and seen the magic in you. He carried you here on his back. And now I have met you and heard the love in your heart. I will carry you on my back to meet the Guardian. I will help you."

"Mama Bear, thank you! You're the best. I knew you weren't a grouchy bear."

"Oho, I will be if I don't get back to sleep soon. Let's go, you Silly Child. Say your farewells."

"My farewells? Wildebeest, you aren't coming?"

"I can't come, Silly Child. Where you are going, only you can go."

"Nor can I.," said Mister Butterfly.

"Oh. I see." I didn't see though. I was actually very sad. "But why?"

"There is no room for us on the rest of this journey. It is up to you now, Silly Child. You must meet the Guardian and find your way home."

There was nothing I could say, or do, to make this any better. "I didn't know you two for very long. But I'm going to miss you both. Will you remember me when I'm gone?"

The Wildebeest didn't say anything. He just looked at me for a long while, in the silence of the cave. The blue fireflies floated around him, making his fur glow even more than usual. Then he took his big cat paw and tapped me on the forehead with it. It was almost like he was patting me on the head. Was he trying to comfort me?

"How could we ever forget such a silly child?" he said.

"We won't. We can't. Remember. The creek will flow on. And one day, it may carry you back here. To us." Mister Butterfly spoke so softly, in that gentle voice he used always. His wings were a soft purple in the light of the cave, and they fluttered as he landed on my hand.

"I'll never forget you. Any of you. Not Mister Fox or Miss Squirrel. Not Mama Ladybug or Ol' Lady Owl. I'll always dream of you, Wildebeest. And I'll think of you the most, Mister Butterfly. Thank you both for helping me. One day I'll help you too. I promise."

Wildebeest raised his paw off the top of my head and smiled. Mister Butterfly flew off my hand and landed on the top of Wildebeest's silver antler. The fireflies gathered underneath them, a blue halo of light that spiraled about them. The little dancing lights flew faster and faster, more of them surrounded my friends. A soft humming filled the cave as they gathered as if the fireflies were singing a song for us. The blue glow got brighter and brighter, and finally, I had to look away. Then the humming stopped, the lights were gone. And when I looked back, so were Wildebeest and Mister Butterfly.

"Where did they go?" I turned and asked Mama Bear.

"Back." was all she said. And then she picked me up in her big paws and placed me on her own back.

"I hope they get home safe."

"Oho, they will. Don't worry, Silly Child. Let's just get you home, hm?"

"Okay, Mama Bear. I'm ready to meet the Guardian."

"And the Guardian is ready to meet you, I'm sure."

I ran my fingers through Mama Bear's golden fur. She slowly climbed out of her cave, and her big steps made me bounce a little on her back. The sunlight made it hard to see as we left the darkness, so I closed my eyes. I closed my eyes and thought of all I'd seen on this Christmas Day. And I wondered what else I'd see before I got home. What was the Guardian like? Where did they live? I raised my face to the sky but kept my eyes closed. The snow fell on my cheeks and melted away. Mama Bear's fur kept me warm.

"Where does the Guardian live, Mama Bear?"

"In the Big Tree."

"I thought Ol' Lady Owl lived in the biggest tree. There's a tree bigger than that."

"Oh yes. Much bigger. Ol' Lady Owl lives on top of the second biggest tree in the forest. But the Guardian sleeps inside the Big Tree."

"How old is the Big Tree, Mama Bear?"

"Oho, good question! Many moons. Many, many moons. All the moons I have seen, all the moons you will see. Add them all together. The Big Tree has seen more moons than that."

"Wow. So... really old."

"Oho yes, Silly Child. Really old."

Mama Bear carried me through the forest. It was strange to go so slow. Especially after flying on the back of Ol' Lady Owl and seeing the forest from the sky. Or moving like lightning on the back of the Wildebeest and seeing the forest become nothing but a blur of color. This was nice though. The blizzard made everything quiet. No more squirrels in the trees or foxes playing in the snow. The blanket of white had covered everything now. If I wasn't on Mama Bear's back, I'd probably be buried beneath it. But she was bigger. Bigger than everything. The snow that would have come up to my neck barely covered her paws.

The swaying and bouncing on Mama Bear's back was very calming too. It made me think of a boat or riding in the car. Riding in the car always made me very sleepy, and this did too. My eyes started to get heavy, and I let out a big yawn.

"You can rest, Silly Child. The walk to the Big Tree is a long one. You have time to close your eyes. Don't worry. We'll get there before the sun starts to set."

"Really? Are you sure?"

"Oho, yes. Don't you worry. Just lay your head down and rest."

"Okay... I'll just close my eyes for a little bit..." And that's what I did. I stretched out on Mama Bear's big back and closed my eyes. Her fur was so soft. It was like sleeping on a giant golden cloud, floating quietly through the sky.

While I slept, I had a dream. A dream of being back home, but also in the forest. Everyone was there too. Mom and Dad, Auntie and Uncle. My cousins, brothers, and sisters were all playing in the living room, where a giant tree was growing. And the animals were there too! Mister Butterfly and Ol' Lady Owl were having a conversation about clouds. Wildebeest and Mama Bear were sitting by the fire, laughing about something. And I was there, in the center, singing my song.

"Silly Child. Oho, Silly Child. Come, wake up now. We're here. The Big Tree."

Opening my eyes and yawning, I looked around. I expected to see my house for a second, but the cold shook me from that dream. That's right, I was still in the forest.

"It was just a dream..."

"Or was it? Oho, don't worry. You'll be back home soon. And I'll be back in my cave. And then we can both take a looong nap. So, are you ready?"

"Ready for what, Mama Bear?"

"To go in. Into the Big Tree. It's time you met the Guardian and went home."

"Where is the Big Tree, Mama Bear?"

"Right in front of you, Silly Child."

"What? I don't see-"

And then I saw it. A pine tree so big that it made Mama Bear look like a mouse. Its trunk was so wide! Wider than three of my houses. And it went so far up that I couldn't see the top. All I could see was a sea of green that hid the sky. I was pretty sure that it even went past the clouds. My mind tried to imagine what the world looked like from up there, but it just couldn't.

"Oh. That's one big tree. I think I see it now, Mama Bear."

"Oho, I'm sure you do. This is the Big Tree. And the Guardian is inside there."

She picked me up off her back and placed me down in front of the Big Tree, and a really big hole in the Big Tree. It was a hollow, like what Miss Squirrel might live in. Except this hollow was big enough for three Mama Bears to walk through while standing on top of each other. It was bigger than Mama Bear's entire cave!

"The Guardian is in there? Why?"

"I never asked them. But when you meet the Guardian, you can ask for yourself. Goodbye now, Silly Child. I hope to see you again one day. Get home safe."

"Wait, Mama Bear!" But she didn't wait. Mama Bear had disappeared into the snow almost as fast as the Wildebeest. I was alone in front of the Big Tree. Could I do this alone? I was only there because of everyone's help. But then I remembered Mister Butterfly's words. "Why bother wondering when the answers are right in front of me? The only way is forward."

The moment I stepped into the hollow, a white light flashed. I couldn't see anything. I was standing somewhere very warm and very quiet. I took a step forward, and the blanket of white moved. It was a fog. Fog so thick that I couldn't see anything! I kept walking forward and trying to push the fog out of my way. The more I walked, the more the fog cleared.

"Hello?" I called out. "Guardian? Are you here?"

"Hello? Hello? Hello?" My voice echoed back to me.

"Is this another cave?" I asked myself.

"No, no cave." A shadow stood in front of me. They weren't an animal, though. They looked human.

"Are you the Guardian?" I asked the shadow, walking closer.

"Are you the Guardian?" They echoed back to me in my voice.

"No, I'm sorry. I came here looking for the Guardian."

"I came here looking for the Guardian." The shadow echoed again, still using my voice.

"I don't understand. Is the Guardian not here?"

The Guardian is here."

"Then where?"

"Here." I was finally close enough to see who the shadow was. And when they turned to face me... It was me.

"I don't understand. Who are you?"

"I'm you." The copy smiled at me, tilting its head.

"You can't be me though. I'm me."

"And so am I."

"Then where is the Guardian? You said the Guardian was here."

"The Guardian is here. Inside of you."

"I don't understand."

"I know. But you are the Guardian. We are all the Guardian. The heart of nature, of magic, that lives in us all. The heart of a silly child. That is the Guardian. You love the forest, don't you?"

"Yes. It's beautiful."

"You love the animals?"

"Yes, they are very nice."

"Then you are the Guardian. We are the Guardian. It's our job to love the forest. To protect it. And to believe in the magic of the forest. You believe, you love, and that makes you the Guardian."

"I still don't get it."

"That's okay, Silly Child. You'll understand one day. Do you want to go home?"

"Yes, please. I just want to go home and spend Christmas with my family."

"Okay, Guardian. Then close your eyes. It's just like the snow, the dead log, and the Spring Grove. Think of home, and you will be home."

"Is it really that easy?"

"For you, Guardian, it is." And then the fog wrapped around me. The copy disappeared, and I was left standing alone in the warm white clouds. It reminded me of that time I spent a day at the hot springs in the mountain. Warm, foggy, and quiet.

But I still didn't get it. I was the Guardian? I had to protect the forest? And I had the power to go home? I tried to walk further, to find more answers, but I couldn't see it. And no more shadows appeared in the fog. Finally, I sat down on the ground, which was wet.

"I'm the Guardian... Think of home... I'm the Guardian. Think of home." I closed my eyes. It felt like days since I'd been back home, even though it was only a couple of hours. 'I want to go home. I want to taste my mom's cookies. I want to play with my cousins. I want to hug my dad. I want to sleep in my bed. I want to watch the fire in the fireplace. I want to go home.'

"Cassie? Are you okay? What are you doing?"

"Are you tired, sweetie?"

"Oh. Papa. Mama. I think I just fell asleep. I'm okay."

"Cassie, Cassie! Come play with us, Cassie. I wanna try your new binoculars. Here, you can try my action figure!"

"Hey, Scotty. Okay, sure. Here you go." Yawning, I pulled my binoculars off and handed them to my cousin.

'Was it just a dream? It all felt so real, though.'

"Cassie, what's that in your hair?"

"Mama?"

My mom leans down and takes something out of my hair and hands it to me. A pine needle covered with a little bit of snow.

"The forest follows you everywhere, huh?" Papa said to me, smiling.

"Yeah, I guess so."

"Come on, Forest Guardian. It's time for dinner."

"Okay!" I climbed out of the chair and stretched. The fire burned beside me, crackling.

"Hey, Mama? Hey, Papa?"

"Yes, sweetie?"

"Merry Christmas."

THE END

Conclusion

Thank you for making it through to the end of *Bedtime Stories for Kids: Christmas Edition*, I hope you enjoyed the stories and was able to provide you with all the everything you need to give your kids the best Christmas tales. Christmas is a beautiful season and one of the most festive. It's alive with family, magic, and love. I hope that this book has brought some of that magic to you and your family. That the characters feel like a part of your family, and that the magic jumps off the pages to fill your home.

There is never a better time of year to sit down and read a story with your kids. With these stories, you and your children can wander away to a Christmas Wonderland together. And by bringing magic into your life, you keep the Christmas magic alive in your own heart. Never stop dreaming. Never stop believing. And never stop wishing on the Christmas Star. Look at the world through the eyes of your children, and you will be happier for it. And your life will be a lot more fun!

The next step is to sit back and relax. Grab yourself a cup of hot cocoa, maybe some cookies. Remember, this is the time of year where you deserve to be with your family. Don't hold back. Enjoy it! And love your family as much as they love you. Merry Christmas! And happy holidays!

Thank you

Before you go, I just wanted to say thank you for purchasing my book.

You could have picked from dozens of other books on the same topic but you took a chance and chose this one.

So, a HUGE thanks to you for getting this book and for reading all the way to the end.

Now I wanted to ask you for a small favor. ***Could you please consider posting a review on the platform? Reviews are one of the easiest ways to support the work of independent authors.***

This feedback will help me continue to write the type of books that will help you get the results you want. So if you enjoyed it, please let me know.